Table of Contents:

Top 15 Amazing Dessert Recipes Collection:

By Ryder Clerk

Recipe No 1: Butterfinger Bars

Ingredients:

- 1 mug adulation
- 1 mug light brown sugar
- 1/2 mug granulated sugar
- 1/2 tablespoon vanilla excerpt
- 2 large eggs
- 2½ mugs each- purpose flour
- 1 tablespoon baking soda pop
- 1/2 tablespoon swab
- 2 mugs Butterfinger Bars about 15 " fun size " bars, coarsely diced

For the Frosting

- 3/4 mug delicate peanut adulation
- 1/2 mug adulation softened
- 1/2 tablespoon vanilla excerpt
- 1½ mugs pulverized sugar

- 1- 2 Soupspoons milk
- 1/2 mug diced butter finger bits about 4 " fun size " bars

How to make:

- ➢ Preheat roaster to 350 degrees F.
- ➢ Add adulation, brown sugar and granulated sugar to a mixing coliseum and cream together until smooth and light. Add the vanilla and eggs and mix well.
- ➢ Add flour, incinerating soda pop and swab and blend on low speed until just combined. Stir in diced Butterfinger bits.
- ➢ Smooth admixture into a smoothly greased 9 × 13 inch baking visage. Singe for 24-26 twinkles, until center of bars are set, and no longer lustrous looking.
- ➢ Remove from roaster and cool fully before frosting.

For the Frosting:

- ➢ Using an electric mixer, beat the peanut adulation and adulation on medium- speed until fully smooth. Add vanilla and blend.
- ➢ Reduce speed to low and add in the remaining constituents, beating until completely incorporated. Increase speed to medium-high and beat the frosting for 1- 2 twinkles, or until light and ethereal.

Notes:

- ➢ **Storage Instructions:** Keep in a watertight vessel in the fridge for over to a week.
- ➢ **Indurating Instructions:** Cool butter finger bars fully also flash snap uncovered for 30 twinkles to harden the frosting. Wrap tightly in plastic serape and tinfoil. Indurate for over to a month.

Nutrition:

- Calories: 367kcal
- Carbohydrates: 46g
- Protein: 5g
- Fat: 20g
- Saturated Fat: 10g
- Polyunsaturated Fat: 2g
- Monounsaturated Fat: 6g
- Trans Fat: 0.5g
- Cholesterol: 46mg
- Sodium: 271mg
- Potassium: 122mg
- Fiber: 1g
- Sugar: 30g
- Vitamin A: 378IU
- Vitamin C: 0.001mg
- Calcium: 27mg
- Iron: 1mg

Recipe No 2: Key Lime Pie

Ingredients:

Graham cracker crust

- 1 ½ mugs ground graham crackers(about 12 full wastes, crushed)
- 1/3 mug granulated sugar
- 6 Soupspoons adulation, melted

Key Lime Filling

- 2 14 ounce barrels candied condensed milk
- 4 ounces cream rubbish, softened
- ¾ mug crucial lime juice
- zest from 2 regular limes, or 4 crucial limes

Whipped Cream Beating

- 1 mug heavy trouncing cream
- 1/4 mug pulverized sugar
- 1/2 tablespoon vanilla excerpt

How to make:

- **Make the crust:** Preheat roaster to 350F. Mix graham cracker motes, sugar, and melted adulation in a small coliseum. Pour scruple admixture into an 8" -9.5" pie visage and press it forcefully in the bottom of the visage and a little bit up the sides of the visage. Singe for 10 twinkles. Remove from roaster and allow cooling.
  For the Filling
- **Make the stuffing:** Add cream rubbish to a mixing coliseum and beat well with electric beaters until smooth. Add both barrels of candied condensed milk, lime juice, and lime tang and blend again until smooth. Pour into set graham cracker crust.
- **Singe** in preheated roaster for 10 twinkles. Allow pie to cool for about 30 twinkles, also chill for at least 3 hours, before serving.
- **Whipped Cream Condiments:** Add heavy cream to a mixing coliseum and beat with electric mixers for 1 nanosecond. Sluggishly add powdered sugar and vanilla and continue beating until stiff peaks form. Spread or pipe the whipped cream on top of the cooled pie.

Notes:

- **Gingersnap Cookie Crust:** Assemble and singe the same way.
- 1 ½ mugs brickle gingersnap cookie motes
- 2 soupspoons sugar
- 5 soupspoons adulation, melted
- **Crucial Lime Juice:** Juice either about 20 small crucial limes, or (recommended) use a bottle of Nellie and Joe's Key Lime Juice.

Nutrition:

- Calories: 444kcal
- Carbohydrates: 54g
- Protein: 7g
- Fat: 23g
- Saturated Fat: 13g
- Cholesterol: 75mg
- Sodium: 242mg
- Potassium: 309mg
- Sugar: 46g
- Vitamin A: 780IU
- Vitamin C: 6.4mg
- Calcium: 222mg
- Iron: 0.6mg

Recipe No 3: Apple Crisp

Ingredients:

Deteriorate Beating

- 2/3 mug old- fashioned rolled oats
- 1/2 mug each- purpose flour
- 1/2 mug light brown sugar
- 1/2 tablespoon ground cinnamon
- 1/2 tablespoon baking greasepaint
- 1/2 mug interspersed adulation, cut into small pieces

Apple filling

- 3- 4 large Granny Smith apples, hulled and thinly sliced
- 3 Soupspoons interspersed adulation, melted
- 2 Soupspoons each- purpose flour
- 1 Teaspoon bomb juice
- 3 Soupspoons milk
- 1/2 tablespoon vanilla excerpt

- 1/4 mug light brown sugar
- 1/2 tablespoon ground cinnamon
- 1/4 tablespoon ground nutmeg

For serving (voluntary)

- Vanilla Ice Cream
- Manual Caramel Sauce

How to make:

- Preheat roaster to 375 degrees F.

Crumble Beating

- In a medium size coliseum combine oats, flour, brown sugar, cinnamon, and incinerating greasepaint. Add adulation and cut in with a confection blender or chopstick until well combined. Chill while you prepare the apple stuffing.

Apple Filling

- I use a Johnny Apple Peeler to peel, core and slice the apples all at formerly. It makes the process a lot briskly.
- In a small coliseum stir together melted adulation and flour until smooth. Add bomb juice, milk and vanilla and stir. Stir in brown sugar, cinnamon, and nutmeg.
- Pour adulation admixture over apples and toss to fleece. Pour apple admixture into an 8 × 8- inch baking dish and spread into an indeed subcaste. Sprinkle deteriorate beating unevenly over the apples.
- Singe for about 35 twinkles or until golden brown and top is set. Remove from roaster and allow cooling for at least 10 twinkles before serving.
- Serve with vanilla ice cream and manual caramel sauce, if asked.

Notes:

- **Make Ahead Instructions:** Make the apple filling as instructed but add an redundant splash of bomb juice to keep the apples from turning brown. Store in an airtight vessel, in the fridge, for over to one day. Make the scruple beating and store independently in the fridge.
- **Indurating Instructions:** Prepare and singe apple crisp as directed. Cool fully, also cover with a double subcaste of aluminum antipode. indurate for over to 3 months. flux overnight in the refrigerator, also warm in a 350 °F roaster for 20- 25 twinkles or until hotted through.
- **Gluten Free Apple:** Crisp Substitute Gluten-free flour and oats.
- **Apple Crisp without Oats:** forget the oats and add an redundant ⅓ mug flour and ⅓ mug brown sugar.
- **Crockpot Apple Crisp:** Place prepared apple filling in the bottom of the slow cooker. Add deteriorate beating. Place a many paper apkins on top of the oat beating, to keep condensation from the lid from making the beating soppy. Cook on high for 3- 4 hours, or low for 6- 8 hours until apples are tender.
- **Dutch Apple pie:** Pour the apple filling into an unbaked pie shell. Add the scruple beating on top. Singe for about 45 twinkles, until apples are tender. Cool for 2 hours before slicing and serving.

Nutrition:

- Calories: 382kcal
- Carbohydrates: 57g
- Protein: 2g
- Fat: 16g
- Saturated Fat: 10g
- Cholesterol: 42mg
- Sodium: 64mg
- Potassium: 235mg
- Fiber: 3g
- Sugar: 38g
- Vitamin A: 560IU
- Vitamin C: 6.1mg
- Calcium: 63mg
- Iron: 1.2mg

Recipe No 4: Snickerdoodle Muffins

Ingredients:

- 1/2 mug unsalted adulation, softened
- 2/3 mug granulated sugar
- 1 large egg
- 1½ ladles vanilla excerpt
- 1/2 mug milk
- 1/4 mug plain Greek yogurt, or sour cream
- 1⅔ mugs each- purpose flour
- 1½ ladles incinerating greasepaint
- 1/4 tablespoon baking soda pop
- 1/2 tablespoon ground cinnamon
- 1/2 tablespoon swab

For Beating

- 3 Soupspoons adulation, melted
- 1/3 mug granulated sugar

- 2 ladles ground cinnamon

How to make:

- Preheat the roaster to 375 degrees F. Spray a standard muffin visage freehandedly with non-stick cuisine spray. Set away.
- Add the adulation and granulated sugar to a large mixing coliseum or the coliseum of a stage mixer. Cream together for about 2 twinkles, until smooth and well combined.
- Add egg. Add vanilla, milk and Greek yogurt and blend until combined.
- Add flour, incinerating greasepaint, incinerating soda pop, cinnamon and swab and fold in using a rubber spatula, just until combined. Don't overmix.
- Ladle batter into set muffin drums, filling each about2/3 full.
- Singe in preheated roaster for about 15- 20 twinkles or until a toothpick fitted in the center comes out clean (or with just a many wettish motes).
- Allow to cool in the muffin drum for a nanosecond or two before removing to a line cooling rack.
- While the muffins singe, melt the adulation for the beating.
- In a separate small vessel blend together the grained sugar and cinnamon.
- Once the muffins are out of the roaster and have cooled for just a many twinkles, use a confection encounter to encounter a thin subcaste of melted adulation over each muffin.
- Sprinkle freehandedly with cinnamon sugar admixture. (You can also dip the muffin tops in the melted adulation, followed by the sugar, but I 've set up that they look proper when you use a confection encounter and also sprinkle the sugar.)

Nutrition:

- Calories: 237kcal
- Carbohydrates: 31g
- Protein: 3g
- Fat: 11g
- Saturated Fat: 6g
- Cholesterol: 42mg
- Sodium: 157mg
- Potassium: 93mg
- Sugar: 17g
- Vitamin A: 360IU
- Calcium: 49mg
- Iron: 0.9mg

Recipe No 5: Chicken Pot Pie

Ingredients:

- 1 pound boneless skinless chicken breasts
- 1/3 mug adulation
- 1/2 mug celery, sliced
- 1/3 mug onion, diced
- 1/3 mug each- purpose flour
- 1/2 tablespoon swab
- 1/4 tablespoon lately base black pepper
- 1/4 tablespoon celery seed
- 1/2 tablespoon garlic greasepaint
- 1 tablespoon More than bouillon base, chicken, or further to taste (or cover 1 bouillon cell)
- 1 mug milk
- 8 ounces firmed veggies (blend of carrots, peas, green sap, and sludge)
- 2 9inch unbaked pie crusts

How to make:

- Preheat roaster to 425 degrees F. Season chicken with swab and pepper. Add the chicken to a large saucepan and cover it with water.
- Bring to a pustule and cook for 6- 10 twinkles or until the chicken is just slightly cooked through. Remove the chicken to a plate, reserve about 1 ¾ mugs of the water in a measuring mug, and discard the rest.
- Add onions, celery and adulation to the saucepan and cook for a many twinkles, until soft and translucent. Stir in the flour, swab, pepper, garlic greasepaint, bullion paste and celery seed.
- Sluggishly stir in the reticent water and milk. Poach over medium-low heat until thick.
- Hash the chicken and add it to the pot along with the frozen vegetables. Taste and season with further swab, pepper, bullion or garlic greasepaint if demanded.
- Pour admixture into nethermost piecrust. Cover with top crust, seal edges, and cut down redundant dough. Make a many small gashes in the top crust to allow brume to escape.
- Singe for 30- 35 twinkles, or until confection is golden brown and stuffing is bubbly. However, cover it with tinfoil, if you find the piecrust is browning too snappily.
- Cool for at least 15- 20 twinkles before serving to allow it to set up.

Nutrition:

- Calories: 201kcal
- Carbohydrates: 10g
- Protein: 15g
- Fat: 10g
- Saturated Fat: 5g
- Cholesterol: 59mg
- Sodium: 326mg
- Potassium: 386mg
- Fiber: 1g
- Sugar: 2g
- Vitamin A: 1770IU
- Vitamin C: 4.3mg
- Calcium: 53mg
- Iron: 0.9mg

Recipe No 6: Pumpkin Mug Cake

Ingredients:

- ¼ mug each- purpose flour
- 3 Soupspoons granulated sugar
- 1/8 tablespoon ground cinnamon
- ¼ tablespoon pumpkin pie spice
- ¼ tablespoon baking greasepaint
- Pinch swab
- 2 Soupspoons milk
- 1 Teaspoon canned pumpkin
- 1 Teaspoon melted adulation
- Gusto vanilla excerpt
- 1 Teaspoon chocolate chips, if asked , or serve with a nugget of whipped cream

How to make:

- Add flour, sugar, cinnamon, pumpkin pie spice, incinerating greasepaint, and swab to a mug and stir together.

- Stir in milk, pumpkin, melted adulation and vanilla excerpt until smooth, being sure to scrape the bottom of the mug. Stir in chocolate chips, if asked.
- Cook in microwave oven for 70- 90 seconds (until cutlet is just set, but still slightly candescent on top). Allow to rest in microwave oven for 1 minute before consuming.

Notes:

- Because all broilers are different, it's delicate to give a precise chef time. Start with 70 seconds, stay 1 minute while it cools, also look to see if it's set. Add a fresh 15- 25 seconds if demanded. Allow it to rest in the microwave oven for 1 nanosecond.
- The trick with mug galettes is to stop cooking the cutlet before than you suppose, because you want it to be soft on the inside, and the cutlet will also continue to cook as it cools.

Nutrition:

- Calories: 452kcal
- Carbohydrates: 74g
- Protein: 5g
- Fat: 16g
- Saturated Fat: 10g
- Cholesterol: 35mg
- Sodium: 127mg
- Potassium: 143mg
- Fiber: 2g
- Sugar: 47g
- Vitamin A: 2684IU
- Calcium: 97mg
- Iron: 2mg

Recipe No 7: Buckeye Balls

Ingredients:

- 4 cups sifted confectioners' sugar
- 1 ½ cups creamy peanut butter
- ½ cup butter, softened
- 1 teaspoon vanilla extract
- 6 ounces semi-sweet chocolate chips
- 2 tablespoons shortening

How to make:

- Line a baking sheet with waxed paper; set aside.
- Place confectioners' sugar, peanut butter, softened butter, and vanilla into a large bowl; mix together with your hands to form a smooth stiff dough. Shape into balls using 2 teaspoons of dough for each ball. Place on prepared baking sheet; refrigerate until ready to coat.
- Melt shortening and chocolate together in a metal bowl over a pan of lightly simmering water, stirring occasionally, until smooth; remove from heat.
- Remove balls from the refrigerator; insert a wooden toothpick into a ball, and dip into melted chocolate. Return to baking sheet, chocolate-side down, and remove toothpick. Repeat with remaining balls. Refrigerate for 30 minutes to set.

Nutrition:

(Per Serving)

- Calories: 204kcal
- Carbohydrates: 22.8g
- Protein: 3.7g
- Fat: 12g

- Saturated Fat: 4.5g
- Cholesterol: 8.1mg
- Sodium: 81.2mg
- Potassium: 103mg
- Fiber: 1.2g
- Sugar: 20.7g
- Vitamin A: 94.5IU
- Calcium: 6.6mg
- Iron: 0.2mg

Recipe No 8: Chocolate Mint Cookies

Ingredients:

- 1 cup butter , softened
- 1½ cups granulated sugar
- 2 large eggs
- 1 teaspoon vanilla extract
- 2 1/4 cups all-purpose flour
- 2/3 cup unsweetened cocoa powder
- 1/2 teaspoon baking soda
- 1/4 teaspoon salt
- 10 oz package Andes creme de Menthe Baking Chips or 9.5 oz bag andes mint chocolates, chopped (about 1 ½ cups)

How to make:

- Preheat oven to 350 degrees.
- In a large bowl cream together butter and sugar until smooth and pale colored. Add eggs and vanilla and beat until mix until incorporated.

- Stir together flour, cocoa powder, baking soda, and salt; add to butter mixture. Stir in mint chocolate pieces, reserving about ¼ cup for pressing into the tops of the rolled cookie dough.
- Spoon and roll cookie dough into desired size (I like mine bigger--about 2-3 tablespoons) Place spread apart on a baking sheet lined with parchment paper or silpat liner. Bake for 10-12 minutes or just until set. (Cookies wont be shiny on top, but may appear slightly soft and will set up after removing them from the oven to cool for a few minutes.)

Notes:

- **Make ahead Instructions:** Make the dough up to 2 days ahead of time and store it in the refrigerator.
- **Freezing Instructions:** The cookie dough balls may be frozen for up to 3 months. Bake from frozen, adding a few extra minutes to the cook time. To freeze the baked cookies, allow them to cool completely and store in a freezer-safe bag for up to 3 months.

Nutrition:

- Calories: 235kcal
- Carbohydrates: 31g
- Protein: 2g
- Fat: 11g
- Saturated Fat: 7g
- Cholesterol: 36mg
- Sodium: 133mg
- Potassium: 54mg
- Fiber: 1g
- Sugar: 21g
- Vitamin A: 290IU
- Vitamin C: 0.1mg
- Calcium: 25mg
- Iron: 1mg

Recipe No 9: Torrijas

Ingredients:

- 1 loaf banal French chuck, sliced into1.5 inch thick slices (about 12- 15 slices)
- 1½ mugs warm milk
- 1 tablespoon vanilla excerpt
- 3 large eggs
- Oil painting for frying(canola or vegetable)
- 2 tablespoon granulated sugar
- 1/2 tablespoon ground cinnamon

How to make:

- Pour the warm milk and vanilla into a shallow coliseum. Crack the eggs into a separate shallow coliseum and beat them well until smooth.
- Combine the grained sugar and cinnamon and set away.
- Pour enough oil painting into a large skillet to cover the bottom of the visage. Turn heat to medium and once oil painting is hot, but not smoking, start cooking the torijas.

- Dip a slice of chuck in the milk on both sides, letting it soak well. also, dip it in the beaten eggs on both sides. Place in the visage and cook, frying and flipping for a many twinkles until golden on both sides.
- Remove to a plate lined with paper apkins or a line rack. Sprinkle with cinnamon sugar (or honey, if preferred).
- Serve warm or chill and serve cold.

Notes:

- **Bread:** I called for french chuck because it's the closest thing I could find to what we used in Spain. Still, you can use a birthstone, challah or brioche chuck. Slice the loaf in thick1.5 inch slices and be sure to let it dry out for a many days on the counter, or toast the slices and let them dry out on the counter for an hour or two.
- **Egg:** You will need roughly 1 egg for every 4- 5 slices of chuck.

Nutrition:

- Calories: 113kcal
- Carbohydrates: 18g
- Protein: 5g
- Fat: 2g
- Saturated Fat: 1g
- Cholesterol: 40mg
- Sodium: 162mg
- Potassium: 80mg
- Fiber: 1g
- Sugar: 4g
- Vitamin A: 94IU
- Calcium: 45mg
- Iron: 1mg

Recipe No 10: Chocolate Peppermint Cake Roll

Ingredients:

For the cutlet

- 4 large eggs, separated
- 1/2 mug ⅓ mug granulated sugar, divided
- 1 tablespoon vanilla excerpt
- 1/2 mug each- purpose flour
- 1/3 mug thin cocoa greasepaint
- 1/2 tablespoon baking greasepaint
- 1/4 tablespoon baking soda pop
- 1/8 tablespoon swab
- 1/3 mug water

For the filling

- 8 ounces cream rubbish
- 1/4 mug adulation
- 1 mug pulverized sugar

- 1/2 tablespoon peppermint excerpt
- 20 starlight mint delicacies crushed

For the ganache

- 1/2 mug heavy trouncing cream
- 1 mugsemi-sweet chocolate chips or 3 oz. semi-sweet baking chocolate
- Starlight mint delicacies, crushed for beating.

How to make:

For the cutlet

- Preheat roaster to 375 degrees F. Grease a 15 x 10- inch jelly- roll visage; line with diploma paper. Grease and flour paper.
- Beat egg whites in large coliseum until soft peaks form; gradationally add ½ mug granulated sugar, beating until stiff peaks form.
- Beat egg thralldom and vanilla in medium coliseum on medium speed of mixer 3 twinkles. Gradationally add remaining ⅓ mug granulated sugar; continue beating 2 fresh twinkles.
- Stir together flour, cocoa, incinerating greasepaint, incinerating soda pop and swab; add to egg thralldom admixture alternatively with water, beating on low speed just until batter is smooth.
- Gradationally fold chocolate admixture into beaten egg whites until well amalgamated. Spread batter unevenly in set visage.
- Singe 14 to 16 twinkles or until top springs back when touched smoothly in center and a toothpick fitted comes out clean.
- Allow cutlet to cool in the visage for ONE nanosecond.
- Lift the diploma paper and hot cutlet out of the visage and onto a flat (heat-safe) face. Incontinently, while the cutlet is hot, starting at one of the short ends, use your hands to gently and sluggishly roll the cutlet (and diploma paper!) all the way over.
- Allow the rolled up cutlet to cool fully, on top of a line cooling rack.(Setting it on a line rack allows it to cool underneath the roll, and keeps the cutlet from sweating).
- Transfer to the fridge to cool for an fresh 30 twinkles.
- While the cutlet roll is cooling in the fridge, mix the cream rubbish, adulation, pulverized sugar and peppermint excerpt together with an electric mixer until ethereal and smooth.
- Gently stir in asked quantum of crushed peppermint delicacies, to taste. Save a sprinkle for smattering on the ganache, at the end, if asked .
- Once the cutlet roll is cooled fully, untwine it veritably precisely. Gently smooth the stuffing in an indeed subcaste over the cutlet.
- Roll up the cutlet, without the diplomapaper. However, to help release it, (If you see it start to stick at all to the paper you can use a adulation cutter gently scrape along the nethermost edge of the cutlet as you roll it up.)
- Cover with plastic serape and chill for at least 1 hour.

For the Ganache

- Heat heavy cream in a saucepan until hot. Pour over chocolate and stir continuously until the chocolate is melted and smooth.
- Allow the ganache to cool for several twinkles to give it time to cake up a little.

- Gently ladle pour the chocolate ganache over the top of the peppermint roll. Sprinkle fresh diced peppermint delicacy on top, if asked.
- Chill for at least 20 twinkles before serving.
- Store in the fridge, covered, for over to three days.

Notes:

- **Make ahead instructions:** The cutlet roll can be set fully and cooled for 1- 2 days before serving. OR, you can singe the cutlet, roll it in the diploma paper to cool. formerly cool, chill it (rolled in the diploma paper) for over to 1 day, before filling and adding the ganache.
- **To indurate:** Prepare the cutlet roll fully, with the stuffing but don't add the ganache. indurate for over to 2- 3 months. Flux overnight in the refrigerator before adding the ganache and also slicing and serving.

Nutrition:

- Calories: 571kcal
- Carbohydrates: 64g
- Protein: 7g
- Fat: 32g
- Saturated Fat: 18g
- Cholesterol: 150mg
- Sodium: 258mg
- Potassium: 302mg
- Fiber: 3g
- Sugar: 48g
- Vitamin A: 905IU
- Calcium: 84mg
- Iron: 2.8mg

Recipe No 11: Peach Scones

Ingredients:

- 2 mugs each- purpose flour
- 1/3 mug granulated sugar
- 2 ladles incinerating greasepaint
- 1/4 tablespoon baking soda pop
- 1/2 tablespoon swab
- 1/2 mug unsalted adulation (1 stick), firmed
- 1/3 mug peach Greek yogurt (I use this kind)
- 1/3 mug heavy trouncing cream
- 1 large egg
- 1 tablespoon vanilla excerpt
- 1/2 mug fresh peaches(about 1 peach), minced

For the Glaze

- 1 mug pulverized sugar
- 1- 2 Soupspoons milk.

How to make:

- Preheat roaster to 400 degrees F. Line a baking distance with diploma paper.
- In a mixing coliseum whisk together flour, sugar, incinerating greasepaint, incinerating soda pop and swab.
- Grate the frozen adulation and add to dry admixture. Use a chopstick or confection blender to cut in the adulation.
- In a separate coliseum whisk together yogurt, cream, egg, and vanilla until well amalgamated.
- Add to the dry admixture and use a rubber spatula to fold the constituents in until it starts to come together in large clumps.
- Stir in the minced fresh peaches. Gently knead admixture by hand (in the mixing coliseum) just a many times until it comes together. Try not to handle the dough too much.
- Dust a clean face with flour and drop dough onto face. Gently stroke and shape into an 8- inch round.
- Cut into 8 wedges also transfer to a diploma lined baking distance.
- Singe in preheated roaster until golden, about 16 – 18 twinkles.
- Cool on a line rack for 10 twinkles before spraying the glaze on top. These are stylish served the day they are set.

  For the glaze
- Add powdered sugar to a mixing coliseum with 1 Tbsp milk and stir until smooth. Add fresh milk, if demanded.

Notes:

- **Mix- sways:** Use plain Greek yogurt and blend in cranberries, blueberries, chocolate chips, or whatever differently you may like.
- **Make Ahead Instructions:** The scone dough can be made, cut, and shaped a many hours ahead of time (cover well and store in the refrigerator).
- **Indurating Instructions:** Scone dough can be firmed for over to 1 month after being cut and shaped. Place unbaked scones on a baking distance and place in freezer for 1 hour to flash snap. Transfer to a freezer safe vessel or bag. Thaw overnight before incinerating. To indurate baked scones, wrap each scone tightly in plastic serape and place in freezer safe bag for over to 1 month.

Nutrition:

- Calories: 525kcal
- Carbohydrates: 86g
- Protein: 8g
- Fat: 16g
- Saturated Fat: 9g
- Cholesterol: 65mg
- Sodium: 182mg
- Potassium: 234mg
- Fiber: 1g

- Sugar: 40g
- Vitamin A: 560IU
- Vitamin C: 0.7mg
- Calcium: 88mg
- Iron: 3mg

Recipe No 12: Chocolate Covered Marshmallows

Ingredients:

- 35 regular size marshmallows, about 1 bag
- 1 bag Caramel Bits, or places, or manual (½ the manual batch)
- 1 bag Ghirardelli incinerating chips (or Chocolate Melting Wafers)
- 18 lollipop sticks.

How to make:

- Line a baking distance with diploma paper. Set away. Secure two marshmallows to each cutlet pop stick or straw.
- Melt caramel according to package instructions. Dip marshmallows in the caramel and curve or use a ladle to help cover them on all sides. Allow redundant caramel to drop off, and place on set visage. Chill for at least 30 twinkles.
- Add chocolate chips or wafers to a microwave oven safe coliseum on 50 power for 1- 2 twinkles, stirring every 15 seconds, until smooth and melted. Dip caramel

carpeted marshmallows in the chocolate. Use a ladle to help smooth chocolate each around. Allow redundant chocolate to drop off, and return to diploma lined visage.

- Refrigerate for 15 twinkles or until chocolate is set. Store leavings in the fridge.

Notes:

Form Variations

- **Like a further:** squeezed the chocolate covered marshmallows between honey graham crackers. It's like a no- chef s ' more and it's succulent!
- **No caramel:** simply skip the caramel way and dip the mallows in chocolate.
- **Add condiments:** once you 've dipped them in chocolate, allow the chocolate to set up for a many seconds and also gently press condiments onto the chocolate, like diced nuts, tattered coconut, sprinkles, etc.
- **Dip apples:** Got leftover constituents? Make caramel/ chocolate apples!
- **Make Ahead Instructions:** Make them several days in advance and store them in a covered vessel at room temperature or in the refrigerator, depending on your climate.
- **Indurating Instructions:** allow to cool and set up fully and place them in a freezer safe bag for 2- 3 months. Flux on counter before eating.

Nutrition:

- Calories: 180kcal
- Carbohydrates: 29g
- Protein: 1g
- Fat: 6g
- Saturated Fat: 3g
- Cholesterol: 4mg
- Sodium: 56mg
- Potassium: 34mg
- Sugar: 25g
- Vitamin A: 55IU
- Vitamin C: 0.2mg
- Calcium: 48mg
- Iron: 0.3mg

Recipe No 13: Overnight Cinnamon Rolls

Ingredients:

Dough

- 2½ ladles active dry incentive
- 1 mug warm milk
- 1/4 mug granulated sugar ½ tablespoon, divided
- 1 tablespoon swab
- 1 large egg
- 1/3 mug unsalted adulation, softened
- 3 ½ – 4 mugs chuck
- flour, or each- purpose

Filling

- 6 Soupspoons unsalted adulation, softened
- 2/3 mug packed light brown sugar
- 2 Soupspoons ground cinnamon

Frosting

- 4 ounces cream rubbish, ½ block softened
- 2½ mugs pulverized sugar
- 6 Soupspoons milk
- 1 tablespoon vanilla excerpt.

How to make:

- **Evidence incentive:** In a mixer add incentive, warm milk, and ½-tablespoon sugar and gently stir. Allow to rest for 5- 10 twinkles for the incentive to "evidence" and the admixture to get sudsy on the top (if this doesn't be, try again with fresh active incentive).
- **Make Dough:** Add swab, sugar, egg, adulation, and 2 mugs of flour to the mixing coliseum. Mix on medium speed until combined. Add another mug of flour and continue mixing. Add further flour as demanded until dough pulls down from the bottom and sides of coliseum. Mix for 5 twinkles. Dough should be smooth and elastic but slightly sticky.
- **First Rise:** Remove dough to a large greased coliseum, cover, and allow it to rise for 1 ½ hours or until doubled in volume.
- **Roll and shape:** Punch dough down and turn out onto a smoothly floured or oiled work face. Roll dough into a 20" x18" cube.
- **Fill and cut:** Smooth adulation over the top of the dough, Mix cinnamon and brown sugar together and sprinkle unevenly over the top, leaving about 1/2-inch border. Roll the dough into a tight "log" and use a sharp saw-toothed cutter or some tooth floss to cut the dough into slices about1.5 elevation thick.
- **Refrigerate late:** Place rolls onto a buttered 9 × 13" or rimmed cookers partial distance (18 × 13"). Cover visage with a lid or tightly with plastic serape and tinfoil and chill overnight, 8- 12 hours. (You could also indurate at this point, if asked. flux overnight in the refrigerator.)
- **Alternate rise:** Remove rolls from the refrigerator and allow to rise until doubled in volume, about 1 ½ – 2 hours. *
- **Singe:** Singe at 375 degrees F for 18- 25 twinkles, until golden and cooked through in the center. Spread frosting over warm from the roaster rolls.

  Cream rubbish Frosting:
- Add cream rubbish to a mixing coliseum and beat with electric mixers until smooth. Add remaining constituents and beat well until smooth. Add fresh milk or pulverized sugar to make the frosting thicker, or thinner, as asked . Smooth frosting over cinnamon rolls.

Notes:

- **Storehouse:** Instructions Store leftover cooled manual cinnamon rolls in a watertight vessel for 3- 5 days. Rewarm collectively in microwave oven for about 15 seconds or until soft.
- **Indurating Instructions:** Ignited rolls can be firmed for over to 3 months. Flux overnight in the refrigerator and warm in the microwave oven for a many seconds.
- Instant incentive to substitute instant incentive skip the first step of proofing the incentive and mix the incentive with 2 mugs flour, sugar and swab before adding that to the stage mixer with water, milk, egg, and adulation.

Nutrition:

- Calories: 259kcal
- Carbohydrates: 36g
- Protein: 2g
- Fat: 12g
- Saturated Fat: 7g
- Cholesterol: 45mg
- Sodium: 235mg
- Potassium: 66mg
- Sugar: 34g
- Vitamin A: 435IU
- Calcium: 57mg
- Iron: 0.2mg

Recipe No 14: Peanut Butter Popcorn

Ingredients:

- 10- 11 mugs lately popped popcorn
  Peanut Adulation Sauce
- 1 mug honey
- 2/3 mug granulated sugar
- 1 mug delicate peanut adulation
- 1 tablespoon vanilla excerpt
- 1- 2 mugs Reese's pieces, voluntary.

How to make:

- Add popcorn to an redundant large mixing coliseum.
- In medium saucepan over medium heat add honey and sugar and stir well to combine. Bring to a pustule and boil for 2 twinkles, shifting.
- Remove from heat and stir in peanut adulation until smooth. Stir in vanilla.

- Sluggishly pour HALF of the warm sauce over the popcorn blend and gently stir to fleece. Dapple further peanut adulation sauce, until your asked coating (you may not use it all, depending on preference). Sprinkle in Reese's pieces, if using.
- Allow to cool for a many twinkles before eating.

Notes:

- Makes about 10 mugs popcorn.

Variations:

- **Fall Party Mix:** After sheeting the popcorn in the peanut adulation sauce, throw in pretzels, delicacy sludge and reese's pieces!
- **Condiments:** After sheeting the popcorn in the peanut adulation sauce, try adding some M&M's, Reese's Pieces, diced Butterfinger, or your favorite chocolate chips!
- **Chocolate Peanut Adulation Popcorn:** After the peanut adulation popcorn cools, mizzle on melted chocolate also let cool.

Nutrition:

- Calories: 350kcal
- Carbohydrates: 55g
- Protein: 8g
- Fat: 14g
- Saturated Fat: 3g
- Polyunsaturated Fat: 4g
- Monounsaturated Fat: 6g
- Sodium: 121mg
- Potassium: 222mg
- Fiber: 3g
- Sugar: 44g
- Vitamin A: 22IU
- Vitamin C: 1mg
- Calcium: 14mg
- Iron: 1mg

Recipe No 15: Strawberry Crepes

Ingredients:

For the blintzes

- 4 large eggs
- 1/3 mug adulation, softened
- 1/2 mug granulated sugar
- 1 mug each- purpose flour
- 11/4 mugs milk
- 1 tablespoon vanilla excerpt
- 1/4 tablespoon swab

For the stuffing

- 2 mugs fresh strawberries, sliced
- 4 ounces cream rubbish, room temperature
- 1/4 mug pulverized sugar
- 1/2 tablespoon vanilla excerpt
- 1 pint heavy trouncing cream

- 3 Soupspoons pulverized sugar.

How to make:

For the blintzes

- ➢ Add all constituents to a blender and mix until smooth. Scrape down the sides of the blender if demanded. Refrigerate batter for 30 twinkles.(Recommended, but not needed).
- ➢ Toast a largenon-stick skillet to medium heat. When skillet is hot, smoothly grease it with a little adulation or cuisine spray.
- ➢ Hold the handle of the skillet and as you pour a many soupspoons of batter in, cock the skillet around in an indirect stir to allow the batter to unevenly cover the bottom of the visage, in a thin subcaste.
- ➢ Cook for 30 seconds- 1 twinkles or until the edges of the waffle coil slightly and the bottom of the waffle is smoothly golden. Flip to the other side and cook for another 30 seconds.
- ➢ Acclimate your heat between medium-medium high until your blintzes are cooking in about 30 seconds on each side. Re-grease your visage every many blintzes, as demanded.)
- ➢ Remove waffle to a plate. Add further blintzes to the plate as you cook them, and cover the plate to keep them warm.

For the stuffing

- ➢ In a small coliseum blend together the cream rubbish, pulverized sugar, and vanilla until smooth.
- ➢ In another mixing coliseum, beat the cream and powdered sugar on high speed until stiff peaks.
- ➢ Ladle utmost of the whipped cream into the cream rubbish admixture and fold in until smooth. Reserve a little bit of whipped cream for beating on the blintzes, if asked.
- ➢ Ladle a thin subcaste of the stuffing onto a waffle. Add some fresh strawberries on top and roll it up.
- ➢ Serve dusted with pulverized sugar, redundant strawberries and whipped cream, if asked.

Notes:

- ➢ **Make Ahead Instructions:** The waffle batter can be made 1 day in advance, stored covered in the fridge. You can also make the cream filling 1 day in advance and slice the strawberries and store them independently in the fridge. Cooked blintzes will keep in the fridge, covered well, for 2- 3 days.

Nutrition:

- Calories: 282kcal
- Carbohydrates: 20g
- Protein: 4g
- Fat: 20g
- Saturated Fat: 12g
- Cholesterol: 120mg

- Sodium: 141mg
- Potassium: 120mg
- Sugar: 12g
- Vitamin A: 805IU
- Vitamin C: 11.5mg
- Calcium: 65mg
- Iron: 0.8mg

www.ingramcontent.com/pod-product-compliance
Lightning Source LLC
LaVergne TN
LVHW080819170826
845678LV00011B/2069

* 9 7 9 8 8 4 8 6 2 4 4 3 4 *